For Piet

A Parents Magazine
Read Aloud Original

Library of Congress Cataloging in Publication Data
Quackenbush, Robert M.   Henry babysits.
SUMMARY: Henry the Duck has his hands full when
all the neighbors bring their babies for him to
watch one day.
   [1. Baby sitting—Fiction.   2. Ducks—Fiction]
I. Title.
PZ7.Q16Hb   1983   [E]   83-2247
ISBN 0-8193-1107-3   AACR2
ISBN 0-8193-1108-1 (lib. bdg.)

HENRY BABYSITS

by Robert Quackenbush

PARENTS MAGAZINE PRESS · NEW YORK

Henry the Duck was enjoying
a quiet day at home
when the doorbell rang.

It was Henry's friend, Clara,
with her baby nephew.
"Would you mind babysitting
for my nephew?" she asked.
Henry was not sure
he knew how to babysit.
"It's easy," said Clara.
"It's my nephew's nap time
and he'll be fast asleep."

Henry said he would be
glad to babysit.
When Clara left, he put
her baby nephew on the couch
and went back
to reading his paper.
The doorbell rang again.

It was Henry's
next-door neighbor.
"I saw Clara bring
her nephew over,"
she said.
"Can you watch my baby, too?
She'll be no trouble."
Henry was a good neighbor,
so he said yes.

As soon as the neighbor left,
the kitten began to cry.
Henry was afraid she would
wake Clara's nephew.
He ran to get some milk
for the kitten.
But he had no milk.
Just then the doorbell rang.

"I heard you were babysitting
this afternoon, Henry,"
said another neighbor.
"Would you please sit
with Baby Amanda?"
Henry saw the bottle of milk
in Baby Amanda's hands,
so he agreed to watch her.

Henry set Baby Amanda down.
He took her bottle and poured
a little of the milk
into a dish.
He gave the milk to the kitten
and the bottle back to Amanda.
Now both babies were happy.
And Clara's nephew
was fast asleep.

Suddenly Baby Amanda
began to cry.
Henry tried burping her,
but that didn't work.
"Maybe she needs changing,"
he thought.
"But I have no diapers."
The doorbell rang again.
It was another neighbor
with another baby.

"I heard you were babysitting,"
said the neighbor.
"Would you please
watch my baby?
He'll be no trouble at all.
He may just need a clean diaper.
When Henry saw
the box of diapers,
he said he would babysit.

In a flash,
Henry changed Baby Amanda
and the monkey, too.
He mopped his brow with relief.
Clara's nephew was
still fast asleep.

Meanwhile the kitten had finished
her milk and wanted to play.
But Henry had no toys.
The kitten started to meow.
Baby Amanda started to cry.
Henry wished he had some toys.

Once again the doorbell rang.
It was still another neighbor
with another baby for Henry.
"Just give him this ball
to play with and he'll be
no trouble," said the neighbor.
Henry took the puppy
and the ball inside.

Quickly Henry tossed the ball
to the kitten and Baby Amanda.
They stopped crying
and started to play.
But the puppy
wanted to play, too.
So he began to chase the kitten.

Round and round the room
ran the kitten and the puppy.
Baby Amanda thought
this was fun.
She began shaking her bottle,
splashing milk everywhere.

The monkey saw Baby Amanda
shaking her bottle.
He thought it would be fun
to throw things.
Lamps and books and flowerpots
went crashing to the floor.

Windows smashed!
Curtains fell!
Henry could not stop
what was happening.

At last it was quiet.
The babies were tired and
they fell fast asleep.
Henry looked around.
Poor Henry.
His house was a mess.

The babies were still sleeping
when the neighbors came
to take them home.
The neighbors thanked Henry
for being such a
good babysitter.

Then Clara came
to pick up her nephew.
She wondered to herself why
Henry's house was such a mess.
But when she saw her nephew
was still asleep she knew
everything was all right.
"You see, Henry," said Clara...

"babysitting is easy."

ABOUT THE AUTHOR

ROBERT QUACKENBUSH is the creator of the popular Henry the Duck series, which includes *Henry's Awful Mistake, Henry's Important Date,* and *Henry Goes West.*

The idea for this latest story came to Mr. Quackenbush when he noticed that his son's babysitter always ended up with more children than she started out with. "That's because she is such a good babysitter. At the end of the day she is very tired," says Mr. Quackenbush, "but the children just love her."

Robert Quackenbush has written and illustrated many books for children. His artwork has been exhibited in leading museums across the U.S. and is now on display in his New York City gallery. He also teaches writing and illustrating there.